**Wonder Mole's Scent Costume Party**
Somos8 series

© Text and illustrations: Pato Mena, 2019
© Edition: NubeOcho, 2019
www.nubeocho.com • hello@nubeocho.com

Original title: *La gran fiesta de los olores*
English translation: Céline Siret
Text editing: Rebecca Packard and Laura Fielden

Distributed in the United States by
Consortium Book Sales & Distribution

First edition: september 2019
ISBN: 978-84-17123-98-7
Legal deposit: M-39104-2018

Printed in Portugal.

Tonight, Wonder Mole is hosting his famous
Scent Costume Party. Where only moles are invited
to such a distinguished celebration.

But wait a minute...
Do you know what a Scent Costume Party is?

Moles live underground, and they can barely see.
To make up for it, they've developed a fantastic sense of smell.

I SMELL A
BEAUTIFUL DAY!

So if a mole goes to a costume party, he doesn't get dressed up like you or me because his mole friends wouldn't see his costume. That's why they came up with an inventive solution:

They wear a scent costume.

OK. You're now ready to
start this book!

# WONDER MOLE'S
# SCENT COSTUME PARTY

Pato Mena

nubeOCHO

"The first guest has arrived! **SNIFF, SNIFF**...
What do we have here?" Wonder Mole asked.
"Oh, a jaguar! What a great costume. I love it!
Please come in!"

"Thank you, Wonder Mole," the first guest replied.

"Wow! A horse! **SNIFF, SNIFF**... and a frog! Such elegant fragrances! Welcome!" Wonder Mole exclaimed.

"Thank you very much, Wonder Mole."

"**SNIFF, SNIFF**... A fox and a crocodile!
What fantastic smells! Come in, come in!"

"Don't mind if we do!" both guests replied.

"Oh, what a surprise! **SNIFF**... A weasel costume! Wow, I've smelled similar costumes at quite a few parties, but yours is surprisingly realistic. It's very scary!" Wonder Mole said.

"Hehehe, thanks!" the clever weasel said, slinking into the party. Luckily for him, moles couldn't see who he really was.

All the guests had arrived and the party was a total hit! Wonder Mole should have been the happiest of all, but the weasel was actually happier because his plan was working. If everything went as planned, he would have two fat moles for dinner.

"Your weasel costume is great," most of the guests said.

"Thank you very much. Let's celebrate by eating loads of food. Let's get fat! Hehehehe..."

But then...

# DING! DONG!

"Inspector! What brings you to my house at this late hour?" Wonder Mole asked, puzzled by the policemole's arrival.

"Sorry for interrupting this great party, Mr. Wonder Mole, but we have heard there is a very dangerous weasel wandering around, and I came to smell that everything was in order," the policemole replied.

"No need to worry,
Mr. Policemole. We are
having a great night."

"I'm glad to hear that, but if
you smell something funny,
let me know."

PHEW!

"Of course. Good night. Hmm... Inspector, wait! Now that I think of it, you should come in for a moment."

WHAT?

"Because you know, tonight we have..."

"Mr. Wonder Mole, like I said, I'm on duty tonight.
So I definitely should..."

ACCEPT YOUR INVITATION!
BECAUSE MY NOSE IS THE SHARPEST IN THE AREA!

"Let the contest begin!"
Wonder Mole exclaimed
amidst the clapping
and cheering.

"And the finalists are: the great giraffe costume!
The bold penguin costume!
And the shocking weasel costume!"

"Judge, you may take a whiff of each contestant," Wonder Mole said.

The policemole first judged the giraffe costume.

**"SNIFF! SNIFF!** Splendid exotic touches...
Very subtle fragrance," he said.

The penguin costume came next.

**"SNIFF! SNIFF!** Incredible! You can even smell the freshness of the polar air with hints of fish. Amazing!"

Lastly, the judge came close to the weasel,
who couldn't stop shaking.

SNIFF SNIFF

"Now this is what I call a real weasel smell. Splendid!"

"Amazing detail! It even has the smell of a weasel's breath."

"Wait a moment," the policemole said...

... what would happen if, at one of your parties, there was a...?"

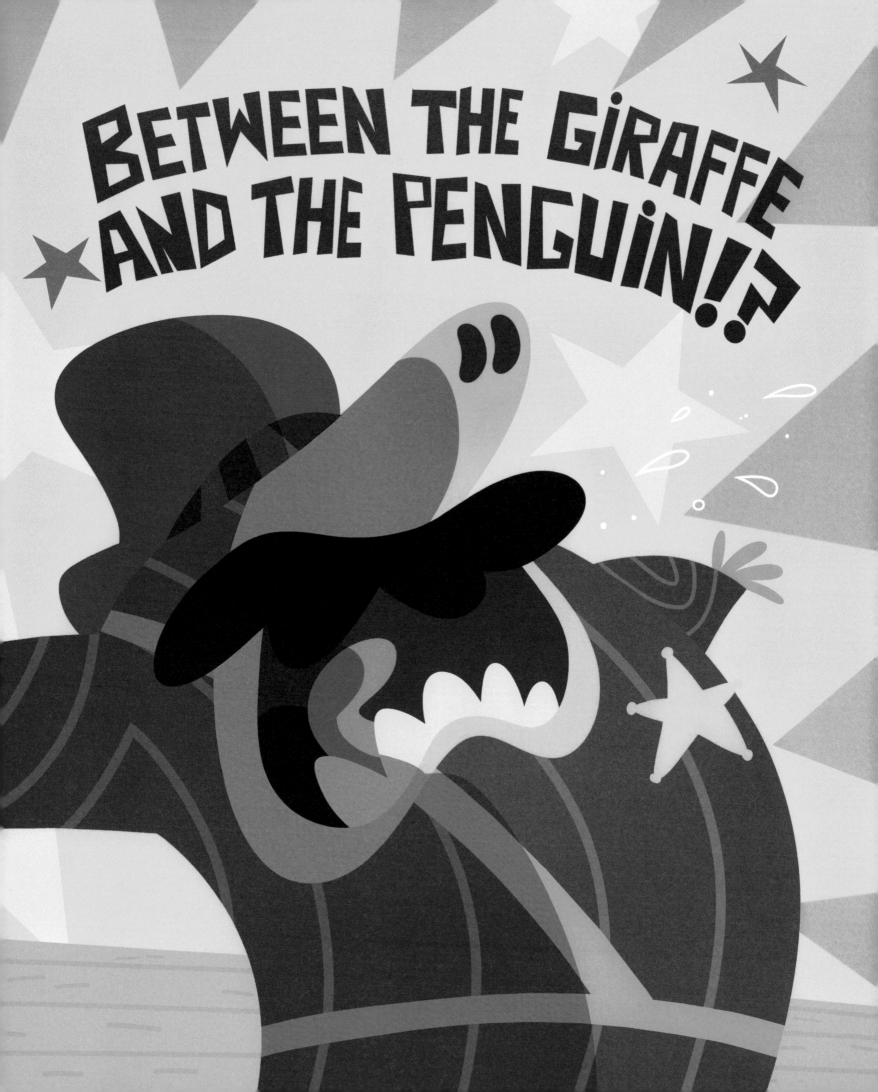

In the midst of the jubilant cheering at the judge's decision, the weasel realized he wasn't going to get his mole dinner after all... But his luck hadn't completely run out. He could still escape if he took advantage of the confusion.

"I'm leaving this crazy house right now!"

But at that moment...

"Good evening, Wonder Mole," a very sleepy hedgehog said. "Could you please turn the music down and tell your guests to lower their voices? I'm having trouble sleeping."

"Please accept my apologies, my dear neighbor. I can assure you we will tone this party down."

"Great! Thank you very much!" the hedgehog replied, saying goodbye.
"Good night Mr. Wonder Mole, good night my mole friends and oh...
I didn't see you there! Good night, weasel!"